WHEN YOU ADOPT A
Pugicorn

D0689348

For my family
—T.B.

First published in 2019 by Hodder Children's Books, Hodder and Stoughton, London, U.K.

ISBN 978-1-338-86523-3

12 11 10 9 8 7 6 5 4 3 2   22 23 24 25 26 27

Printed in the U.S.A.   40

First Scholastic printing, September 2022

The art in this book was created digitally.

Text by Matilda Rose
Illustrations by Tim Budgen
Book design by Katie Messenger
Cover design by Heather Kelly

WHEN YOU ADOPT A
Pugicorn

Haven for Magical Pets

Haven for Magical Pets

OPEN

MAGICAL PETS INSIDE!

by **Matilda Rose** • illustrated by **Tim Budgen**

SCHOLASTIC INC.

Next time you're in Fairyland, make
sure you pay a visit to Mrs. Paws's Haven for Magical
Pets in the town of Twinkleton-Under-Beanstalk.
It's a truly enchanting place.

There are baby dragons, talking llamas,
beautiful phoenixes, and even playful starwhals.
But the most magical pets of all . . .

fairy

fairy
Bakes

... are the unicorns.
Every year, young princesses and princes
arrive in their carriages to pick a perfect
unicorn pet. This year was no different.

First came Princess Mia.
She chose friendly Flutter Toes.

Prince Alfie chose
shy Glitter Horn,

and Princess Ruby chose
stylish Mellow Curls.

Last to arrive was little Princess Ava. "I'd like a
unicorn, please. With sparkly hooves, a rainbow-colored
mane, and a very, very, very long and swishy tail."

"Dear me!" said Mrs. Paws, the shop's owner. "It looks like we're
all out of unicorns. But don't worry, I have just the thing . . ."

"Oh!" said Ava. "What is it?"

"It's **Pugicorn!**" said Mrs. Paws.

Pugicorn was small and round, with a funny snuffly
nose, a curly little tail, and a rainbow-colored horn.

Hmm, thought Princess Ava.
Pugicorn wasn't quite what she had in mind.

But Ava had an idea. "Guess what, Pugicorn?
I'm going to turn you into the best unicorn ever.
You'll just need to . . . 'think unicorn'!"

But "thinking unicorn" didn't help Pugicorn
keep up at the Galloping Gala.

It didn't help him sit still at the Fairies' Garden Party.

Pugicorn definitely wasn't "thinking unicorn" on his way home from the Mane and Tail Salon . . .

or at Prince Party-Pants's Pet Show.

And as for leaping over rainbows? Nope. No chance.
"You're the worst unicorn ever!" said Princess Ava.
"I'm going to the Unicorn Picnic, and you're not invited."

So Princess Ava stomped off to the Enchanted Forest,
leaving poor Pugicorn all alone.

A little rainbow tear fell down Pugicorn's cheek.
"Thinking unicorn" does not come naturally when you're a pugicorn.

At first, Princess Ava had a wonderful time at the picnic, playing Unicorn Hoopla, watching the Unicorn Rainbow Race, and petting the unicorns' flowy manes.

I wish I had a unicorn, Ava thought longingly.

But soon, Ava began to miss Pugicorn. Her friends' pets were graceful and elegant, but none of them were short and round and the perfect size for snuggling, and while swishing tails were pretty, Princess Ava missed a certain curly little tail. "I think we should go since the sun is setting," Ava said to her friends. She was eager to get home before dark.

But everything looked
different in the dark.
Which way was the palace?!

"This way?" asked Princess Mia.
But Flutter Toes didn't want to
get her dainty hooves muddy.

"Down here?" asked
Prince Alfie. But Glitter
Horn refused to tangle her
mane on the nasty,
prickly branches.

"Through these trees?" suggested Princess Ruby. But an owl hooted loudly above them, and Mellow Curls swooned with shock.

HOOT!

You see, unicorns may look dazzlingly beautiful, but they're absolutely no good in a crisis.

Then, just when they thought things couldn't get
any worse, the panicking princesses and princes
heard a rustling, snuffling sound deep in the forest.

"A MONSTER!" shrieked Princess Ruby.
"What if it eats our confetti cakes?" said Princess Mia.
"What if it eats *us*?" squeaked Prince Alfie.

The sound came closer . . . and closer
. . . and CLOSER, until . . .

"Pugicorn!" gasped Ava.

Her loyal little pet had come to save them,
rainbow lights shining from his magical horn.
A creepy forest was no match for
plucky little Pugicorn!

Together, the princesses, princes, and their unicorns
followed Pugicorn as he led them home . . .

. . . squelching — *slip! slop!* — through the mud . . .

. . . stepping carefully over
the prickly bramble bushes . . .

. . . and leaping — *whee!* — across the stream.

Safely back at the palace, Ava gave
Pugicorn a tummy rub, and she even let him
chew on her second-favorite slipper.

"I'm sorry I tried to change you," said Ava.
"You're not a unicorn. You're Pugicorn—
my Pugicorn—and that's much, *much* better!"

Pugicorn's horn glowed with happiness.

So everyone in Fairyland lived happily ever after:
princesses, princes, Pugicorns, and not-so-perfect unicorns.

And Mrs. Paws's Haven for Magical Pets had never been busier.

The most wished for, longed for pets in Fairyland?

Pugicorns!

Matilda Rose lives in London with her family and two fat pugs named Will and Harry.

Tim Budgen is the rising-star illustrator of *Only One of Me*, *As Nice as Pie*, *Puss in Boots*, and a string of other picture book and novelty titles. He lives in England with his wife and their pets, Baxter and Alfie.